Flatulent Tales

The Adventures of Gilbert the Farting Mouse

(Fourth Edition)

by

R.O. Dent

(Alias Michael Davies)

Illustrated by Holly Cox

© The Mickie Dalton Foundation

November 2009

Flatulent Tales

First Printing October, 2009
Second Edition January, 2011
Fourth Edition December, 2018

ISBN: 978-0-6484702-8-1

Published by The Mickie Dalton Foundation
NSW
Australia

www.mickiedaltonfoundation.com

Dedicated to all the stallholders and musicians

at the Coffs Harbour Harbourside Markets

who make each Sunday such a fun-filled

occasion

The Adventures of Gilbert The Farting Mouse

1. In Which We Meet Gilbert Who Takes a Space Trip

Gilbert was really a very happy mouse. At school, he'd worked hard and graduated near the top of his class and then went to live in his home town of Coffs Harbour where he'd been born. He liked Coffs Harbour. It was a very pretty town and lots of tourists came there, so life was a lot of fun watching all the different people having a good time.

Gilbert found a really fine place to live. It was a drain pipe in a small park right near the beach, nicely sheltered from the wind and rain and he lined it with all the leaves that fell off the trees so that it was really very comfortable indeed.

What made it so special and perfect for a small mouse was that every Sunday, there was a market in that park and people put up stalls to sell lots of different things. Gilbert liked to wander around and have a look at some of the stuff, like the paintings of beaches and lakes that one couple did, or the stone animals like Kookaburras and kangaroos and crocodiles. And one bloke called Kris made and sold didgeridoos and sometimes he played that for the tourists and when he played the really big didgeridoo, the ground trembled and Gilbert liked to dance around as his feet vibrated and tickled.

But what was the best thing of all was that some of the stalls sold food. Gilbert was up and about as the people started arriving, and the smell of coffee made him hungry and there was always lots of

food. One stall sold meat pies, sausage rolls and nachos, another one cakes and tiny pancake balls with syrup, and then there was the Indian food stall that sold curry and samosas, while next to that, two Japanese ladies made fresh sushi, chicken terriyaki and other delectable Japanese dishes, and what was so wonderful that there were always bits dropped around the stalls as well as morsels that fell off the meals that the tourists and visitors bought.

So Gilbert developed a most sophisticated taste for a mouse, and could choose between Indian curry on the rice that fell around, or sushi (and he decided that his favourite was smoked salmon sushi with avocado) or mince meat and puff pastry from the sausage rolls.

But one astonishing day that changed his life, Gilbert was up near the didgeridoo stall dancing to the sound of the smaller instrument when he saw something drop off the table at a stall he hadn't checked out before. It was small and white, and Gilbert cautiously advanced and gave it a sniff and decided this was something especially delicious. He carefully chewed a bit off, and it was nutty and fragrant. Gilbert was curious. What *was* this possible new addition to his already exotic diet? He walked away from the stall, carefully dodging the feet of the tourists who were piling into the market as the sun rose and it got warmer, then looked back to read the stall sign. It said *"Macadamia Nuts."*

Now Gilbert had heard of Macadamia nuts at school and his parents had once talked about them, saying how delicious they were but tended to cause gas, but he hadn't understood that, but he did agree that these nuts tasted wonderful. Caution abandoned, Gilbert scoffed down the rest of the macadamia nut, licked his lips with delight and decided this was really the *BEST!* And then he found a second nut!!!

He grabbed the nut in his teeth and galloped at full speed, scampering behind the stall that sold kids' clothing and the one that sold leather belts and made a beeline for his home, the drain behind the toilet block.

Once inside his home, he settled down on a pile of leaves, determined to make a really special occasion of this. First he sniffed at the nut, deciding he'd been right the first time, it smelled *delicious!* Then he licked the nut all over and finally took a bite, nearly weeping with joy at how delicious it tasted. He chewed slowly like his parents had once told him, savouring every crunch and made it last a full half hour before he got to the last tiny crumb and regretfully decided it was finished. He decided that life was really very good indeed for a small mouse living by the beach in a pretty town like Coffs Harbour and settled down to go to sleep.

But that night, he woke up, feeling something was wrong. His tummy felt tight, almost painful, it was so full it stuck out like a blimp and the pressure was getting worse and worse. He tried turning over, but that didn't help, he got up and walked around the drain pipe, and that did nothing to ease the discomfort and he began to get a bit worried when suddenly he farted.

THRRRRRRRRRRRRRRPPPPPPPPPPPPP!!!!

This was no ordinary fart. It was a huge fart, a *majestic* fart, a fart so enormous that it blew all the leaves out of the drain pipe in a vast cloud and spread them over the grass over a metre away. It increased the pressure inside Gilbert's home that his ears ached for a second or two and rattled the plates in his cupboard. The roar that accompanied the thunderous great fart caused shock waves around the park so that even the cicadas went silent and the birds woke up on their branches and flew around in bewilderment before settling back to sleep again. But Gilbert's discomfort had gone, his tummy was back down to normal size again and he was able to lie down. Quickly racing outside and gathering some leaves back into the drain for his bed, he settled down and went peacefully to sleep, dreaming of the next Sunday market when he might be able to get some more macadamia nuts to eat.

On Sunday morning, Gilbert woke up feeling excited. He got up, brushed his teeth and made his way to the place where the macadamia nut stall was being set up. Taking his place by the tree roots where he was hidden from sight, he settled down and waited to see if his luck would be in. By ten, no nuts had fallen and Gilbert was getting worried. But suddenly he saw a nut drop to the ground, in fact several nuts as a small bag got torn. Gilbert saw his chance. He raced over to the stall and counted three nuts! Gilbert felt that all his birthdays and Christmas had come at once! He attacked the nuts and forgot all about chewing carefully and slowly, he just scarfed those nuts down and he must have eaten three or four before he saw the stall holder walk back to his table and sit down.

Gilbert tried to run back to his drain. But he wasn't able to run very fast, he found in dismay, his tummy was so huge that he feet couldn't really touch the ground and he felt the same pressure building up that he'd experienced the previous Sunday, but this time it got worse, really worse, horribly, *horribly* worse and Gilbert began to wish he could fart again and relieve the pressure.

His wish was granted.

Gilbert farted.

THRRRRRRRRRRPPPPPPPPPPPPPPPP

And whatever had happened the previous time, it was nothing like this fart. This fart was humungous, it was earth shaking, it even made the didgeridoo playing seem soft. It made the leaves shake all over the park and startled seagulls on the beach. The roar of the fart eclipsed the sound of the band playing in the middle of the market and made dogs start barking.

And Gilbert took off into the air. He went straight up, so high and with such speed that a light aeroplane coming into land at Coffs Harbour airport was seriously buffeted around and made the pilot abort the landing. Yachts on the water found their sails suddenly filled so much that they accelerated really fast and the wash added to the surf and sent some surfer dudes flying right over the beach to land in the park. And Gilbert kept going up. The sky got darker and darker and the air got colder and thinner and Gilbert realised he'd gone into orbit!   He looked down and saw he was passing over the North Island of New Zealand. Gilbert was so astonished he didn't feel frightened at all. Even in the cold and thin air, he was fascinated by the experience and the views he was getting. He kept flying past New Zealand and over massive oceans. As he twisted his neck to look around, he farted again and this must have made a course change, because the next land he saw was a big set of islands that he decided must be Hawaii. Before long, because he was heading east, night fell quite suddenly and he began passing over land again, because he could

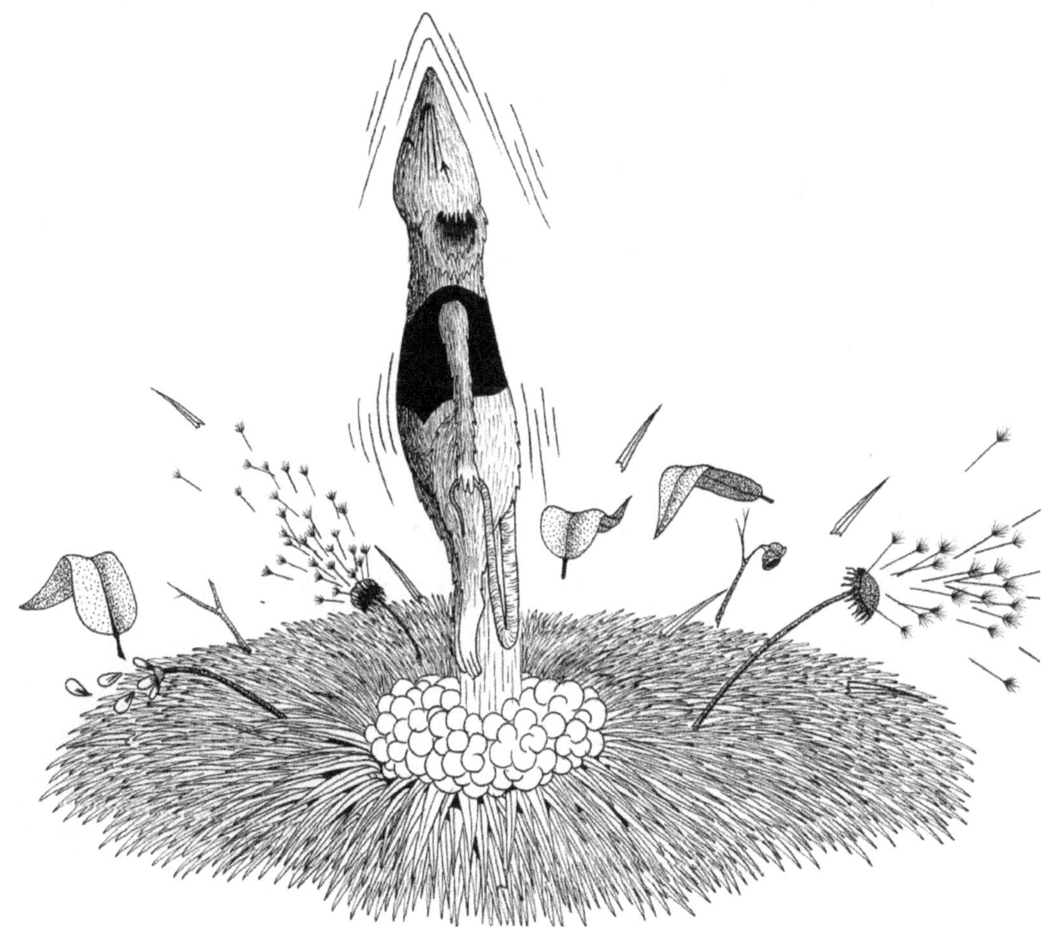

see city lights below him, and he decided that must be North America. More dark underneath without any lights, so he thought he was probably over the Atlantic, more lights and he was passing over Europe. Gilbert realised he was flying really, really fast and began to worry about how he was going to get back to Earth again. As he flew into the rising sun, heading over the Middle East he remembered how the NASA Space Shuttles came down.

Being a very athletic little mouse, Gilbert threw himself into a back flip and succeeded in getting himself looking back at the direction from which he'd come. He took a deep breath and let out another rip-snorting fart.

THRRRRRRRRRRRRPPPPPPPPPPPP!!!!!!

This slowed him down, just like the shuttles did when they fired their engines facing backward, and Gilbert dropped out of orbit and began heading to the ground.

But he still had a long way to get down and he kept travelling round the earth, over India, Thailand, Singapore and Indonesia and suddenly he recognised Australia! He hurtled over the West Coast, over Alice Springs. But he was still high and as he flew over the East Coast he saw Sydney on one side and Brisbane on the other and just about worked out where Coffs Harbour would be, but was too high and he was back over the ocean before he could work out exactly where he was.

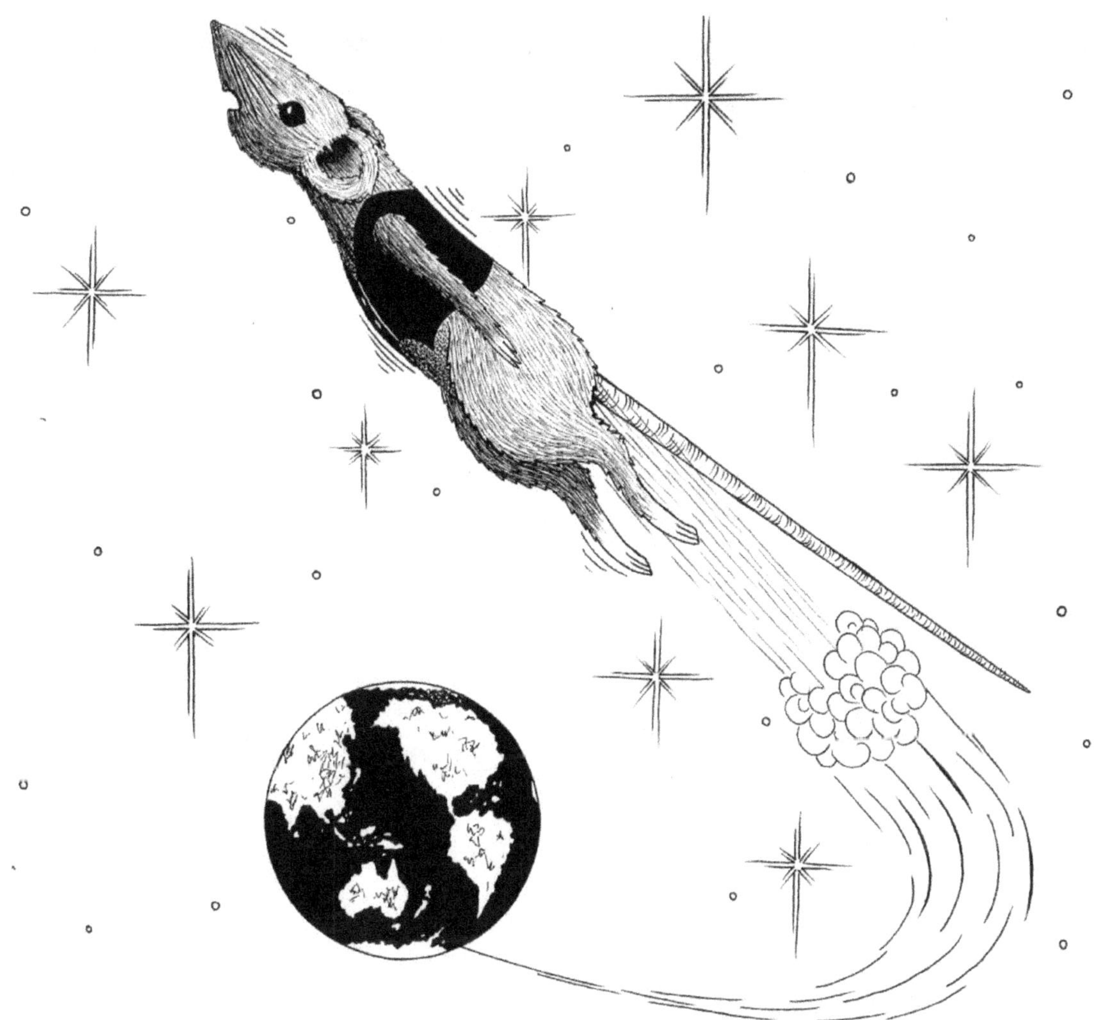

And then, *PLOP!* He was in the ocean! It was probably just as well too, because the heat of the re-entry into the atmosphere had made his rear end really hot and some of the fur was glowing bright red. But he plunged so deep that things got dark, and he realised he needed to get back to fresh air again and quickly before he ran out of breath. Remembering his new talents, he used the last of the gas in his tummy and farted firmly *THRRRRPPPPP!!* and that propelled him up to the surface and back into the air for quite a few metres before he dropped back into the water.

But he realised that he was still a long way from home and he began to feel frightened.

2. In Which Gilbert is Saved by an Octopus

"Well, at least I'm back on Earth," Gilbert said, "but I have no idea of where I am.   I know Australia must be *thataway,* so I'd better start swimming."   And with that he started paddling with all four feet heading back west towards the Australian coast.   Now Gilbert was a pretty good swimmer. He'd once come third in the NSW State Mouse Swimming Championships in backstroke and he was quite strong at freestyle too, so he wasn't too worried. He swam freestyle for a bit and then turned onto his back and swam backstroke for a while, but after a couple of hours of this, he really did begin to feel rather tired and he was also getting quite hungry and having wishful thoughts about smoked salmon sushi and Indian curry and sausage rolls and meat pies and... macadamia nuts.   *Especially* macadamia nuts.

But just as he was starting to get seriously worried, he felt a very soft touch on his shoulders (he was swimming backstroke at the time) and although he thought that it should have frightened him, it didn't, because he sensed somebody very friendly was there. The touch got stronger and he was gently lifted up a bit above the water and he looked round and saw a *HUGE* eye looking at him. It was in the middle of a big grey head and then he saw another eye, just as big.

"Hello!" said a voice. "I'm Karen. I'm an octopus. What are you doing out here? You're a long way from home, aren't you?"

Gillbert realised he was being held up by one of Karen's tentacles. "Hello," he said. "I'm Gilbert and I come from Coffs Harbour, which is somewhere over there. And I've just circled the earth in orbit!" And he told Karen the entire story of how he'd come to fly into orbit and go round the world and then come down in the ocean. "Wow!" said Karen, obviously highly impressed. "I've never been anywhere except just around these parts in the Pacific Ocean. I've always wanted to travel!"

"But can you help me get home?" Gilbert asked.

"I'm sure I can," Karen replied. "But first we need to get you some food and back to dry land. Hang on, just let me rise up a bit."

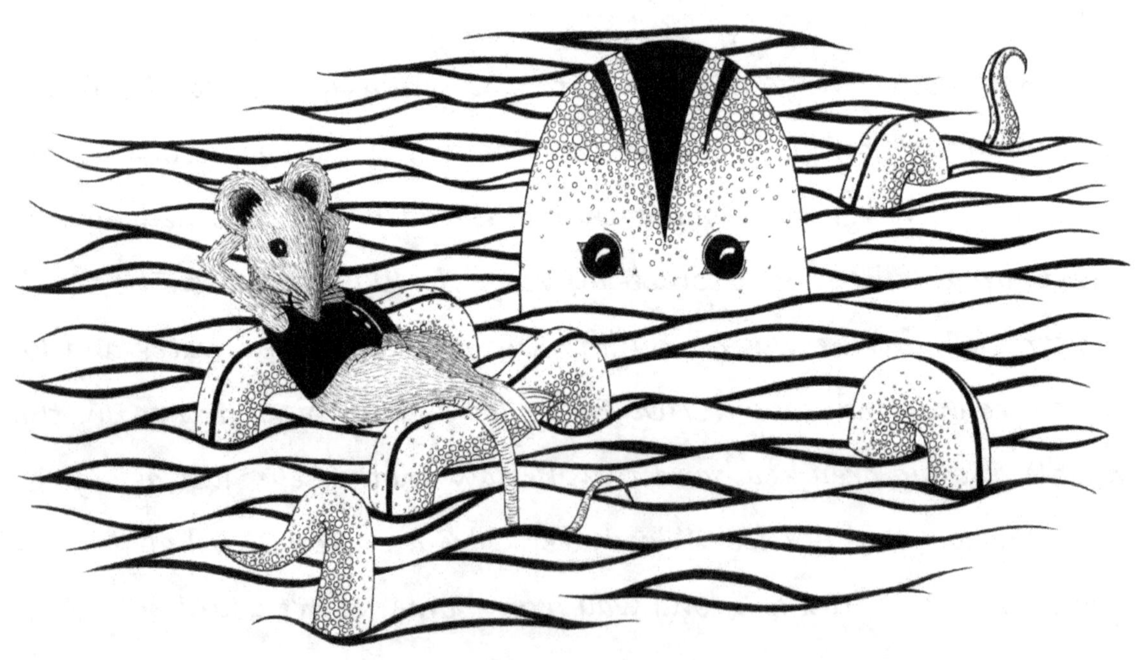

And keeping the tentacle on which Gilbert was sitting just above the surface, she paddled her other tentacles hard downward and raised herself a good metre above the surface.

"Aha!" she said, letting herself back in the water. "I see something!" And she began moving quite fast and Gilbert realised she was propelling water behind her, just the way he shot air backwards with his farts, and they moved along the surface like a ship in sail until Gilbert saw a big brown object floating very close. It was really gigantic compared to him and he realised it was a coconut!

"Hop onto that, Gilbert," said Karen, "that'll keep you afloat without any problems," and she moved her tentacle so that Gilbert could jump onto the floating nut and it floated easily with his weight on it.

While it was a huge relief to Gilbert to be out of the water and onto a firm surface, one thing was still a worry.

"I am really hungry," Gilbert said to himself. "Really, *really* hungry. I haven't eaten since early this morning, and it's got to well into the afternoon by now. If this thing is some sort of nut, I wonder....." And with that he started gnawing at the hard shell and it was hard going, but he gnawed and he gnawed and he gnawed until finally he broke through and out of the hole he'd made came flowing a beautiful cold stream of coconut milk! Gilbert was ecstatic because he was also extremely thirsty and this milk tasted quite delicious. He drank for quite a while the milks stopped gushing out and he resumed nibbling at the shell to make the hole bigger and at last he got to the nut itself. It was wonderful! It was almost as tasty as macadamia nuts and Gilbert happily settled down to filling his empty tummy. He worked his way round the middle of the nut and then when a sudden wave hit it, the coconut broke into two equal halves, leaving Gilbert sitting in the middle of one them, like a circular boat. His tummy had got quite full again and he began to feel that perhaps he'd overdone it, because the pressure inside of him was building rapidly.

"Hey, look over there!" sang out Karen who was bobbing along accompanying Gilbert, and with another free tentacle waved over into the distance. Standing on his hind legs in the middle of the coconut, Gilbert was able to see over the edge and saw the wonderful sight of the Coffs Harbour Jetty.

"I knew it was there, somewhere," said Karen. "If you can get there, you'll be right!"

Gilbert wondered if his new abilities would help, and anyway, the pressure was getting higher and higher and he knew he'd have to give this a go. So he climbed up to the edge of the nut, and parked his rear end over the side, pointed his nose at the island in the distance and let rip.

THRRRRRRRRRRRPPPPPPPPPPPP!!!!!!

It was another *TITANIC* fart. The coconut shook under the strain, the acceleration nearly threw Gilbert off his perch, but he hung on. Behind him, the sea was churned up into a small tidal wave, and Karen who was right there behind him shouted **"Phewaor!"** and disappeared under the waves holding her nose. But Gilbert had no time to worry about Karen, he was grimly holding on and trying to steer the circular boat in the right direction, shifting his little bum as he tried to correct the course and at last he made it, driving the coconut almost half way up the beach, so powerful was his fart propulsion. Finally it hit a shell and turned over, spilling Gilbert on to the sand, but he didn't mind because he was feeling a bit seasick and needed to rest in the warm sun.

But when he woke up, he saw that he was quite close to his beach house near the market. Wearily, he trudged up to the front door, climbed onto the sand bed and fell asleep again, as suited a mouse who had just flown round the world.

3. In Which Gilbert Protects the House

Having discovered his amazing talent and just how invaluable it could be, Gilbert decided he'd better be able to use it when needed but also that it had to be controlled. He didn't want to let out a major-league, rip-snorting, windows-shattering fart,

THRRRRRRRPPPPPPPPPPPPPPPPPP!!

when he was in somebody's house, for instance, that would be considered very rude indeed. Or perhaps when he went to see a film, that would be very disrupting also. Gilbert loved sneaking into the movie house in Coffs Harbour when he knew a good film was showing. He'd first done it, creeping in through the fire doors when they were opened for an airing after a show, sleeping in one corner until the movie started and then leaving when all the crowds had gone and he could safely exit through the fire doors again. He made sure he never missed anything with Russell Crowe, because he was a local boy who lived just down the road in Nana Glen. Once, he'd been there when the management showed old cartoons and he'd seen a Mickie Mouse cartoon and he'd laughed himself silly in his little viewing corner, even letting out just a tiny fart *thrrrppp* because he was so helpless.

So Gilbert searched up and down the Market one Sunday until he found a scrap of canvas and some string and he carefully made himself a compact little bag that he could wear on his back, just big enough to keep a couple of Macadamia nuts with him. He started to collect the nuts whenever he could find some loose ones, because he didn't really like opening up a bag from the stall table, and slowly he accumulated a nice stockpile of nuts in his home in the drain by the toilet block. So from then on, he never left the drain without slipping the backpack on and carrying two Macadamia nuts with him. It was always best to be prepared for any eventuality that might need his amazing talents, he thought.

One day, he was having a chat with a friend of his, Percy the Pooping Potoroo. Percy was known that way because he really didn't care where he pooped (like all Potoroos) and while that was okay when he was outdoors, Potoroos loved creeping into the houses of people whenever they could and finding whatever food had been left lying around but leaving a stinky mess behind.

"It's great, mate!" Percy said to Gilbert. "Those people leave all sorts of stuff lying around. It's best when there's a party or they have guests for dinner, because they all get too tired to clean up afterwards and they go to bed absolutely rat-arsed drunk. I've had steak, chicken, barramundi, you name it, I've scarfed it!"

Gilbert was very impressed, because he'd never eaten steak or Barramundi, though he'd had chicken occasionally when the Japanese ladies dropped some from their chicken teriyaki dishes, or the Indian stall left some curried chicken lying loose after cleaning up at the end of the day. His mouth watered at the idea of the other stuff.

"There's a house just past the railway line," said Percy the Pooping Potoroo. "I found a way in there a few days ago and there's just a couple of young blokes living there. They must be rich, 'cos they have lots of parties with piles of good stuff being served, but they're really scruffy erks and they only clean up a couple of days after the parties, so I'm living high, mate, I tell yuz!"

"Wow!" said Gilbert, mightily impressed, salivating at the idea of feasting on steak and chicken and barramundi and even more delicacies that he'd never heard of.

"Hey, they're having a party tonight!" Percy said. "I heard them talking about it this morning. Why don't you come in with me and see what we can eat?"

That idea struck Gilbert as being totally awesome, so that evening, after it had got dark, Percy the Pooping Potoroo met Gilbert at the railway crossing and they set off just past the restaurants, Percy bounding on his two rear legs like Potoroos do to the house that Percy indicated. Once, Gilbert would have thought of it as a very long way, but now, to a mouse who had farted his way in orbit round the world and across the sea to a desert island half-way to New Zealand and down to Tasmania, it was just a short stroll.

The sounds of the party were already loud as Percy led Gilbert round to the side to a little hole in the wall where the brick had crumbled, leaving a gap big enough for a mouse and a Potoroo to creep through. It came out in the pantry by the kitchen and Percy jumped up onto a shelf and looked through a gap in the serving hatch.

"They're really into it!" he said. "Come and have a look."

Following Percy's tracks and carefully avoiding the little poops that Percy had already left on the pantry shelves, Gilbert peered through the gap. Percy was right, the whole room seemed stuffed full of people, all eating and drinking and the noise was huge. Gilbert started salivating at the smells that reached him.

"We'll have to wait till it's over," Percy said behind him, pooping some more small poops onto the shelf. "But they're all pretty legless already, so it won't be long. And most of them will head off to another party, anyway."

Sure enough, it was only ten o'clock by the clock on the wall that Gilbert could see, and somebody shouted "Let's all go to Jacko's place! He and Bluey are having a party as well!" And within ten minutes the house was empty.

"What a stroke of luck!" said Percy. "Let's get out there!" And leaving a little pile of poops on the shelf, he jumped to the ground, raced out of the pantry to the room where the party had been going just minutes before and leaped onto the table.

Percy bounded on two legs, like a tiny kangaroo and attacked a plate that was full of little pastry puffs with various things on them. "PRAWNS!!!!" he shouted and began scarfing down the puffs, leaving a trail of poops as he moved round the plate. Gilbert took his time, not sure where to start, but being a mouse, the smell of cheese was overwhelming. He found the source of it and sniffed cautiously, because it wasn't ordinary cheese, but creamy, with a white crust on it.

"It's Camembert!" shouted Percy from where he was simultaneously stuffing prawns into his mouth and pooping poops on the plate. "It's French!"

Gilbert licked at the cheese and found it amazingly delicious, creamy and rich. So he took a few mouthfuls then moved away to check out some other plates. He could hardly believe his luck. He ate ham slices, some chicken wings, decided he didn't like paté but he did like olives, left the prawn plate alone because it was almost full of Percy's poops and sipped at a spilled glass of champagne which fizzed on his tongue and made him feel giddy.

Feeling dangerously full, Percy and Gilbert retreated to the pantry and found a spot in one corner for a nap. Gilbert fell asleep almost immediately, but not before letting out a few small, happy little farts, **thrrrppp**; thrrrppp; *thrrrrrrrpp*.

But a noise suddenly woke them.

"What's that?" whispered Gilbert, feeling frightened. "Have they come back already?"

"Not likely," replied Percy. "If they go out to a party, they never get back before dawn." He jumped up to the spyhole that looked out onto the party room. "I think it's burglars!" he whispered. "Come on, let's check!"

He jumped down to the ground, followed by Gilbert and they ran into the party room. Sure enough, there were two men moving round the room, carrying sacks into which they were putting the silver trophy cups that were on one bookshelf, a laptop computer that had been left on the desk and one was disconnecting a dvd player from the really big television in the lounge room.

"What are we going to do?" hissed Percy, spraying poops around in his panic.

Gilbert knew that the situation called for desperate measures. Although already feeling great pressures in his little tummy, he decided greater ammunition was called for. He pulled his knapsack off his back, opened it up and pulled out one lovely, creamy, juicy macadamia nut. Not bothering to take a preparatory lick, he just bit straight into it, chewed and swallowed fast, feeling the pressures building up even more.

"Get in front of me and hold tight!" he called to Percy who by now had almost covered the floor with panicky poops. As soon as Percy was safely ahead of him, Gilbert took a position by a pillar, faced it, and with his rear end directed at the two burglars, let rip with just about the biggest fart he had ever made. It was a colossal fart, an earth-shaking fart, a fart that shook the house, rattled the windows so badly that two of them were blown out of the frames and landed with a smash in the garden outside and set off the alarms of the cars parked in the street.

THRRRRRRRRRRRRRRRRRRRRRRRRRRPPPPPPPPPP!!!

The effect was amazing!

Both men were blasted against the wall, but in trying to regain their balance, they slipped on the thick floor covering of Percy's poops and they banged hard on the wall, collapsing in a heap and banging their heads again on the floor as they went down. They lay silent, unmoving.

"I think they're out cold," said Percy, leaving his safe place and sniffing cautiously at the men's faces.

"We should probably get out of here," said Gilbert, already hearing the sounds of police sirens approaching. "I think we've woken the whole place."

Not bothering to find the way out through the hole in the wall, they jumped out of the empty window frame and hid behind a tree in the front garden. Sure enough, a police cruiser arrived, lights flashing and siren going, but the sound was switched off as the car stopped.

Two large cops raced out of the car to the house, walked round it cautiously until they came to the smashed windows. One stuck his head in.

"Oh, *PHEW!!!*" he shouted. "What a pong!" He stood further back, but shone his flashlight through the empty window frame. "Hey, there's a couple of blokes in there! We'd better get them out!"

Trying to wave clean air into his face, he climbed in and then realised that the two men were not the house tenants but were carrying the bags of stolen goodies.

Percy looked at Gilbert. "Great stuff," he said. "I think we've done our civic duties. Time to get out of here!"

And with that, they returned to the market ground and to their respective homes. Feeling thoroughly relieved from the monstrous fart that had saved the house from being burgled, Gilbert fluffed up the leaves of his bed and went back to a peaceful slumber.

3. In Which Gilbert Saves Somebody from a Fire

It was the time of the floods that ran through Coffs Harbour and left the main road under a couple of metres and peoples' houses were flooded, offices were under water and lots of people were in danger. Gilbert had been forced to abandon his drain home by the toilet blocks because it was quite seriously under water, the whole field where the market took place was flooded and he had found temporary living space in a storage cabinet in the Sailing Club, because it was above the flood waters and he had been able to locate a gap in the flooring big enough for him to get in.

Food wasn't all that plentiful because the kitchens of the club were very careful about food disposal and storage, but there was nobody at the club for a long time while the floods blocked the road to the harbour, so Gilbert was able to gnaw open a small package of cheese and some nuts and he hoped that would last him until things returned to normal.

But one morning he was astonished to hear somebody calling his name from outside. It was a man's voice and this baffled Gilbert. First, why was a human calling for him? And how did he know where Gilbert was?

He jumped up on a table by the window of the dining room and cautiously stuck his nose to the window. He looked out onto the paddock where the market was held and that was under deep water.

But by the steps leading to the Sailing Club entrance, there was a small boat tied to the banister of the steps. And standing in the boat was a man in a police uniform and he was calling Gilbert's name!

"Hey, Gilbert!" called the cop. "I know you're in there, we saw you on the closed circuit security cameras! We need you to help us! It's urgent!"

Quite baffled, Gilbert raced round to the wall where he had his entrance gap and pushed himself out and round to the top of the stairs where the boat was moored.

"Ah, there you are!" called the cop. "Thanks for coming. Gilbert, we really do need your special talents. There's a bloke stuck on the top floor of an office building in town and we can't get the fire-truck with the extending ladders to it, the water's too deep. I think you're the only one who can help us."

Rather nervously, Gilbert made himself jump off the deck and into the boat and he hid under the seats where there seemed to be a lot of coiled rope and a huge ball of string.

"Bewdy, Gilbert!" said the cop went to the back of the boat and started up the outboard motor, unhitched the boat from the banisters and soon they were roaring along the river that was usually the road from the beach into the town. Gilbert had never been in a motor boat before and soon his curiosity overcame his nervousness and he crawled out from under the seat up onto the prow and stood leaning against the side of the boat, enjoying the wind passing through his whiskers.

After about fifteen minutes, the boat reached the main street of Coffs Harbour and the cop coasted to the junction next to a tall building, tied the boat to the traffic light and switched the engine off.

"Look up there, Gilbert," he said, pointing to the top floor of the building. A window had been opened and there was a man standing there, leaning out and waving at them. "Like I said, we can't get the ladder truck here and there's no space to land a chopper on the roof. And I'm worried that a fire could break out, there's been some smoke already. Can you get up there with a rope?"

"But I haven't had any of the right food," Gilbert protested. "I don't know if I can generate enough force to get up there on my own, never mind carrying a heavy rope!"

"We thought of that," replied the cop and opened his side pocket, pulling out a small bag of macadamia nuts and laying out two on the seat beside him. "Will they help?"

"Better make it three," replied Gilbert and began gnawing on the nuts. "But," he said after a few moments demolishing one nut and starting on the second, "I still don't think I can haul all that rope up there."

"No worries," said the cop taking out a third nut and putting it with the last crumbs of the first two as Gilbert polished them off and attacked the third one. "That's why I got that big ball of string. "I'll tie one end to the rope, so if you can get up there with the string, the bloke can then pull up the rope. Think you can do that?"

"Give me a few seconds," said Gilbert, "let me get the nuts working." And with that he started jumping up and down and turning cartwheels and soon his little tummy, which had reduced quite a lot after the last few days of limited food, began to swell and he began having difficulties moving.

While he was doing that, the cop had unwound a long section of string and tied one end securely to one end of the coil of rope then he made a small loop at the other end.

"Okay, Gilbert?" he asked and Gilbert nodded and staggered to the cop who put the loop round Gilbert's neck and shoulders.

Just then, they heard a huge shout from the man at the top of the building.

"Fire!" he shouted. "Fire! Fire!"

"Better get a move on, Gilbert," said the cop.

Gilbert took a careful sighting on the man at the window, took a deep breath and let everything blow! He farted one humungous, bellowing fart and took off with a roar, string unwinding behind him as he shot up the side of the building.

THHHHHHHHHHHHHRRRRRRPPPPPPPPPPPPPP!!!

Behind him, the waters of the flood almost parted, bits of road and pavement appeared briefly before become under water again,

windows in all the surrounding buildings shook and rattled, waves from the flood began racing along the main street before becoming calm again about half a kilometre away and the cop let out a massive shout.

"PHEWORRRR!!! Oh mate! Gilbert! That's disgusting! Oh mate, I don't get paid enough for this, honest!"

But Gilbert saw none of this or heard the cop's yell, he was streaking up the side of the building and he judged it neatly, looping inside the open window and landing on the carpet by the man's feet.

"Gilbert, am I glad to see you," said the man, breathing hard. "Here, let's get that string off you." He pulled the string off Gilbert's shoulders and began pulling upward until he had the end of the rope in his hands. He looked around the room and finally chose the legs of a massive wooden conference table to tie the rope to. He pulled it a few times, made sure it was firm, then climbed onto the window ledge.

"Coming, Gilbert?" he asked. "Why not hitch a ride in my shirt pocket?"

Seeing that was a big enough pocket, Gilbert jumped onto the man's lap and up to his shoulders, then dropped comfortably into the shirt pocket.

"Let's go!" said the man. "Look at that! We're just in time!"

Gilbert looked at the other end of the room and saw smoke billowing in under door.

"Better move!" the man called, and began lowering himself down the rope. He must have been an expert and very fit, Gilbert thought, because he lowered himself smoothly and quickly down the rope and was soon safely in the boat.

"Well done," said the cop and started the outboard engine, motoring smoothly away until they reached the edge of the flood where they let the man get off near his home.

"Thanks again, Gilbert!" said the man. "You're a credit to Coffs Harbour!"

With a wave, he walked off and the cop started motoring again.

"Back to the Sailing Club?" asked the cop.

"Please," replied Gilbert.

"What that bloke said," the cop suddenly spoke as they motored along the river. "I'll second it."

"Well, thank you, Officer!" said Gilbert as they reached the Club stairs again.

Gilbert jumped off the boat onto the deck.

"Hey, Gilbert!" said the cop as he prepared to move off. "You may need these!" and he lobbed the bag of macadamia nuts to Gilbert and they dropped by his side.

Waving at each other, the cop motored off and Gilbert carried his bag of welcome nuts back into the Sailing Club, feeling very good about his day's work.

5. In Which Gilbert Breaks the Sound Barrier

One day, while Gilbert was having a quiet Saturday morning in his little beach house made of sand, he was astonished when he heard a voice calling from the front door. He peeked his head round the doorway of the lounge and saw a strange sight.

It was another mouse, but not like any mouse Gilbert had seen before. For a start, he was wearing a white laboratory coat like a dentist or a scientist. And for another, he had on big horn-rimmed glasses.

"Hello!" said the strange mouse. "I was hoping to catch you in, but you weren't in your regular house in the drain, so I thought I'd try here."

"Who are you?" asked Gilbert, a little annoyed at having his privacy disturbed.

"Let me introduce myself," replied the other mouse. His accent sounded strange to Gilbert, who although he had flown round the world in orbit and down to Tasmania, had never been to any other country, so he couldn't tell what the accent was.

"I am Professor Werner von Braunmaus," said the bespectacled one. "I am the Director of the Fart Propulsion Laboratories in Wagga Wagga, and I would very much like to talk to you."

"Oh!" said Gilbert, rather astonished. "You'd better come inside."

"Thank you," said Professor Braunmaus and followed Gilbert into the lounge room. There was no furniture in the room, but Gilbert had piled up some sand and shaped it into a pair of armchairs.

"We at the FPL have been following your adventures with great interest," said the Professor when they had both settled down. "We have been developing fart propulsion for some years, experimenting with various food products to see which provides the best propulsion, and we have built several experimental devices to enable an ordinary fart to give propulsive power, but we have never encountered such natural abilities as you have displayed."

"I'm very honoured," Gilbert replied, being naturally a polite little mouse. "I hadn't realised I was unique."

"Well, you are," said Professor von Braunmaus. "So we were wondering if you would come and visit us at the Fart Propulsion Laboratories and help us with some developments there?"

"I'd be delighted," said Gilbert. "But how do I get to Wagga Wagga? And how did you get here anyway? It's a very long way!"

"It's been really hard yakka," the professor said. "It's taken three days, using the best Fart Propulsion we have available right now. Come outside, let me show you."

Getting up from the sandy armchair, the professor led Gilbert outside to the sand of the beach where they were hidden from the human world by part of the sea wall. And to Gilbert's amazement, there was a little aeroplane, a very oddly shaped aeroplane indeed. It had a short fuselage with just room for two seats, and the wings were quite long, but hanging on each wing was what looked like a huge engine. But as he walked up to the engine, Gilbert saw there was nothing inside, just some frames, certainly no engine.

"The engines are over here," said the professor and pointed a couple of metres away and there, leaning on the seawall were two rather large, muscular mice, looking extremely weary.

Gilbert was baffled.

"It's the first prototype of the Braunmaus Fart Jet X-1," explained the professor. "Those two mice there are very expert and potent farters but they don't have anything like your ability. They climb inside the engine compartment, hang onto the frames and let rip and that's enough to get us airborne and fly a few kilometres. So it took us several days to get here."

"Well, I'm sure I can help us do it a bit faster," said Gilbert. "But your engines look like they need a rest and some fart food."

"We're hoping you can give us some of what you take, have a night's rest and leave in the morning," said the professor.

So Gilbert led all of them to his drain home where he had a stash of macadamia nuts.

"Just have a little bit now, some more before you go to bed, then we'll have a solid helping in the morning before we take off."

So the party spent the day in Gilbert's drain house, went to sleep and the next morning, Gilbert asked each of them to carry a macadamia nut back to the beach and they sat down by the aeroplane. "Start slowly," cautioned Gilbert, "and we'll increase the consumption as we go. Follow my lead."

The professor didn't eat as he would not be helping the propulsion, but the other three mice scarfed down all four nuts they had brought over and when they had finished, Gilbert suggested that the two other mice should squeeze into one engine space and he would take the other one. They waited until they all started to feel the effects, their tummies distended and almost unable to walk, Gilbert ordered everybody into their places. When they were all settled, with the professor strapped at the flying controls in one of the seats inside the fuselage, Gilbert called out:

"Okay, guys! Deep breath, one, two, three.....Full Throttle!!!"

And indeed, they all let rip together.

THHHHHHHRRRRRRRRRRRRRRRRRRRRRRRRRRRRRRRRPPP!

THHHHHHHHRRRRRRRRRRRRRRRRRRRRRRRRRRRRRRRRPPP!

from the two other mice in one engine slot, and on the other, Gilbert's

THHHHRRRRRRRRRRRRRRRRRRRRRRRRRRRRRPPP!

Even with two professionally trained farting mice on one side, Gilbert still produced more power than they did, so the take off was a shade uneven. But the Fart Jet X-1 lifted off the sand, hurtled into the air and climbed sharply in the direction of Wagga Wagga. Behind them, they left a storm. Sand blew all over Gilbert's house, over the road and into the parking lot by the sailing club. The trees bent in the gale and thousands of seagulls screamed in alarm and flew out to sea. The storm set off alarms in people's houses and police cars began leaving the station and heading to the beach, sirens blaring, while all the tourists and visitors took cover anywhere they could. But nobody was hurt and everything settled down quickly.

"This is *AMAZING!!!*" shouted Professor Werner von Braunmaus. "We've reached ten thousand feet and we're already two hundred kilometres on track! We can get home with just one more fart in about twenty minutes."

And that's how it happened. Twenty-five minutes later, they were down to two thousand feet when Gilbert called for one more deep breath and a concerted trio of farts were emitted:

THHHHHHRRRRRRRRRRRRRRRRRRRRRRRRRRRRRRRRRPPP!

THHHHHHHHRRRRRRRRRRRRRRRRRRRRRRRRRRRRRRRRPPP!

on one side and Gilbert's

THHHHHRRRRRRRRRRRRRRRRRRRRRRRRRRRRRRPPP!

The explosive thrust caused some clear air turbulence to be reported by airline pilots flying over western New South Wales and Air Traffic Controllers instructed pilots to avoid the region for the next thirty minutes though meteorologists were quite unable to explain what had caused the disturbance. But it caused rain to fall over Narromine and strong winds blew down some hay stacks in Parkes near the radio telescope.

But the Braunmaus Fart Jet X-1 had returned to ten thousand feet and was now only a hundred kilometres from Wagga Wagga. In a smooth glide, they completed the rest of the trip and landed at the Fart Propulsion Laboratories airstrip just fifteen minutes later.

Looking a little unsteady, the professor showed Gilbert to his room. "We'd like to do some tests first," he said. "So have a break and we'll start in half an hour."

Not really liking the sound of doing some tests, Gilbert had a quick nap, and was ready to follow the professor to a medical room where he was prodded and poked, examined all over and asked lots of questions about his diet, his history and all about his parents. Gilbert went along with all of it, but already he was missing his drain home, his sandy beach house and his friends like Percy the Pooping Potoroo back in Coffs Harbour as well as the nice scene around the market. But he was curious about what the professor had going here, so he decided to hang around.

"Now," said Professor Werner von Braunmaus. "We are ready for the main tests. Please come with me, Gilbert." And he led the way out to the centre of the entire complex and there was a huge area, many times the size of the markets at Coffs Harbour, more like a giant football field. And running all the way round in a massive oval shape was what looked like a railway track.

"This is our main propulsion test," said the professor. "And here is the test rocket."

Gilbert saw a little trolley with four wheels mounted on the track. It had a sharp nose with a windshield in front, a strong seat behind the windshield and there was something strange sitting on the back behind the seat. It looked like a sphere of metal but with a little indent at the front of it, and at the back, there was a jet outlet.

"That is our Fart Reheat Device," said the professor. "How it works is that you place your rear end against that indent, and when you fart into the cylinder, it ignites the spark plug, it injects some inflammable gas into the cylinder, it expands the fart gas and it all blasts out through the jet, massively increasing the power of the original fart."

"Wow!" said Gilbert, mightily impressed. "Let's try it."

"We'll first try without the Fart Reheat Device to see how fast you can go with normal power," said von Braunmaus. "Let's get you strapped in."

And so Gilbert was strapped, belly down on the trolley, rear end facing the back.

"Let 'er rip!" shouted the professor, and Gilbert did, with a monstrous fart from his earlier snack of macadamia nuts.

THHHHHRRRRRRRRRRRRRRRRRRRPPPPPPPP!

And the trolley shot off with incredible acceleration, raced at mind-boggling speed round the track, once, twice, and kept going. Gilbert kept his head down and the howling wind passed over him because of the windshield, but his little ears were a bit buffeted. It was nowhere near as smooth as when he had flown solo, but he put it down to the all the interference of the trolley he was riding. He kept racing round and he'd done it three times before coming to a halt back at the start. Gilbert looked around and saw that a couple of huts had collapsed, the fence round one corner had fallen outward under the force of the gale and alarm sirens were still going off all around the compound.

"Good Heavens!" exclaimed von Braunmaus. "I have never seen the trolley move so fast or go so far! Let's try it now with the Fart Reheat Device."

So Gilbert moved himself a little so his rear end was positioned comfortably in the indent in the metal cylinder and chewed on a section of macadamia nut to recharge his strength. Meanwhile, Professor von Braunmaus made sure the compound was ready and was speaking into the public address system.

"Attention, Attention! Full Fart Reheat Test about to commence! Hang on to something fixed and put all loose objects away under cover!"

He came back to Gilbert, checked he was ready. "I am switching on the Fart Reheat Device," he said. "You can go any time you're ready."

Gilbert heard the faint hum of the device behind him and knew it was on, so he took a deep breath and let loose just a mid-range fart so as not to apply too much pressure.

THHHHHHHRRRRRRRRRRRRRRRRRPPPPPP!

The trolley took off, racing round the track though not quite as fast as the previous time, but then Gilbert heard the ignition set off behind him and

KERRRRRRRRBLOOOOOOOOOOWIE!!

Gilbert accelerated like he had never done before and he heard the roar of the rocket engine thundering and he went faster and faster until suddenly........ everything went quiet. The wind smoothed out though it kept racing past him, the noise of the rocket engine vanished and Gilbert realised he had exceeded the speed of sound and had broken through the sound barrier. He was going so fast, the only thing keeping him on the rails was that it was angled at the bends so that he didn't fly off. He kept going and going round the track, but as he started to get dizzy, he realised he was slowing and finally he came to a halt.

The professor came and helped him un-strap. "I think that proves the Fart Reheat device really works!" said von Braunmaus with delight.

"In that case, I think I'll go home," said Gilbert. "My job is done."

"No it's not," snapped the professor. "We need you here for a long time yet, we have lots of new developments for you to test."

"But I want go back to Coffs Harbour," complained Gilbert.

"Well, you can't! Guards! Take Gilbert to his room and makes sure he stays! Keep hold of him at all times outside so he doesn't fart his way out of here!"

In horror, Gilbert realised he was a prisoner at the Fart Propulsion Laboratories in Wagga Wagga. He was hustled back to his room by two big white mice and he heard the lock turn as he fell onto his bed, starting to weep a little with loneliness and homesickness. But after a while, he got up and started looking round his room to see if he could find a way out. There was not a lot in the room, just his bed, a chest of drawers and a chair, not even a radio or a television. On the wall, there were two pictures. One was a map of New South Wales and he stared longingly at the location of Coffs Harbour, thinking of his nice little home in the drain by the market toilets and of his beach house made of sand. Next to that was an overhead picture taken from quite high up of the Fart Propulsion Laboratories and he could clearly see the location of the vast railway oval on which he had just exceeded the speed of sound. With a surge of interest, he saw there was a compass on the map, and that the far side of the oval pointed directly at Coffs Harbour. A plan started to form in Gilbert's mind.

The next morning, the door was unlocked and the two big white mice escorted Gilbert first to the canteen then back to the rocket trolley where Professor Werner von Braunmaus was waiting.

"I hope you had a good breakfast?" sneered the professor. "You have a lot of work to do today."

Gilbert said nothing, but he had indeed had a humungous breakfast, gorging as much as he could of bacon and scrambled eggs and sausages with toast and coffee after. To his delight, there had even been a saucer of macadamia nut spread, just like the one sold at the Coffs Harbour market, and Gilbert had scraped all of it into his pocket.

Gilbert was strapped into the trolley again, his little rear end seated comfortably on the indent of the reheat cylinder and he was soon off again with a fart that he deliberately made just a little less forceful than the one with which he had started the previous day.

THHHHRRRRRRRRRRRRRRRRRRRRRRPPPPPP!

The trolley set off and within a few seconds, the ignition cut in and *KERRRRRRRRBLOOOOOOOOOOWIE!!* He accelerated past the speed of sound, round the first bend, then second and onto the far straight, hurtled round the first bend and as he did so, Gilbert realised the trolley was skidding a little outward on its rail. He kept on whistling past the second bend, back into the home straight, round the two bends and back into the far straight and that was when Gilbert initiated his brilliant plan. He had earlier picked the macadamia nut spread from his pocket and now he gulped it down and let out two carefully calibrated farts.....

Thhhhrrrrrppppppppppp and then again, and even finer one *Thhhhrrrrrppppppppppp* and the trolley accelerated again, screamed up to the first bend and this time it skidded so much that it flew off the rails, into the air and kept flying at nearly twenty percent faster than the speed of sound. The sonic boom was heard all round Wagga Wagga, bringing out the residents wandering if a bomb had gone off to signal a terrorist attack and they all milled around in great confusion and police cars set off their sirens and raced around in all directions, windows broke and smashed onto the ground and all the livestock on the farms started running into each other and broke down fences as they tried to run away.

And Gilbert kept on climbing at about twenty degrees, hurtling towards Coffs Harbour and soon he reached nearly thirty thousand feet. In only a few moments he could see Sydney on his right, he recognised the Harbour and the shape of the Opera House and as he slowed and started to descend again, only another few minutes later he could recognise Newcastle and the coast and he knew he didn't have long to reach Coffs Harbour. And at last, in the distance he could see

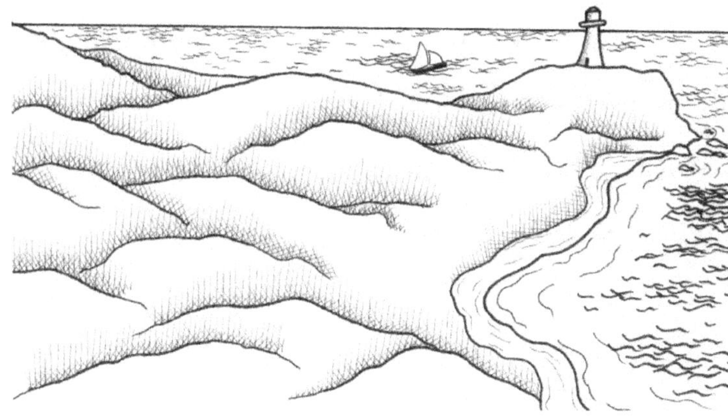

home! He was able to undo his straps and let the trolley fall down below and behind him and repeated his slowing technique that he had used when he went into orbit. He flipped onto his back so he was facing the way he had come, took a breath and let out a fairly low-level fart *Thhhrrrrrrpppppppppp* that was enough to slow him down for the last few hundred feet and with perfect timing, he landed with a splash in the surf just by the sailing club jetty at Coffs Harbour.

"Hello!" said a familiar voice. "What are you doing here in the water again?"

It was Karen the Octopus! "Well, g'day!" exclaimed Gilbert in delight. "I was just passing and I thought I'd drop by!"

And as Karen gently floated him on one tentacle back to the beach, Gilbert told her about his adventures of flying to Wagga Wagga in the Werner von Braunmaus Fart Jet X-1 and travelling faster than sound on the Fart Reheat Device trolley and how he escaped.

"Good on yer, mate!" said Karen. "That'll teach the little prawn to try one on you!"

"Cheers, Karen," said Gilbert as he hopped off the tentacle and set off for his home in the drain. "See you next adventure!"

With a wave of one tentacle, Karen vanished under the surface and Gilbert raced homeward in time for lunch.

6. In Which Gilbert Meets Edna and Ethelred, the Vegetarian Pythons

The week started in a very frightening way for Gilbert. Quite late on the Sunday evening after the market had packed up and everybody had gone home, Gilbert took a stroll round the paddock, mostly for the fresh air and the exercise and because he like the sound of the surf in the evening. He also looked for some different foods, because much as he liked macadamia nuts, too much of a good thing could get boring and he fancied a change. He found a lovely chunk of curried chicken from the Indian food stall and a strand of bacon from the hamburger stand and he was carrying them back to his home in the drain by the toilet block when he heard sounds of squealing from a lot of creatures in the distance. He thought he'd better set off rapidly for home and he had just reached the doorway when he saw what was causing the noise.

RATS!!!!!

Lots of rats, probably fifty or sixty big, heavy rats with enormous teeth and narrow beady eyes. Gilbert hated rats, they were ugly and they smelled bad and they ate anything, including mice. His heart beating with fear, Gilbert jumped inside his drain and rapidly piled as many leaves as he could up against the doorway, praying that they would block out his scent and the smell of the food and nuts he had in there. The sounds of squealing were reduced a lot by the leaves and they must have succeeded in covering the smell of food too, because after about ten minutes the noise faded completely. Trembling with the shock of the danger, Gilbert finally pulled some leaves down from the entrance and made his bed, but it was quite some time before he calmed down enough to fall asleep.

In the morning he woke up and decided it would be safe enough to take a morning stroll, so he left his drain home and walked into the fresh morning air. It was a wonderful morning, mild and sunny even this early in the day, and the surf was just loud enough to be heard, so it was perfect for a small mouse to take his exercise.

But then Gilbert got the second horrible shock. He heard a slithering sound in the grass and he stopped, but then he saw the thing that mice hate above all else, the thing that frightens them almost into a heart failure.

SNAKES!!!!!

And there were two of them, two huge, hideous diamond-back pythons that must have been well over two metres long, *and they were looking straight at Gilbert!* Letting out a shriek of fear, Gilbert set off at a full-pelt run back for his house and with a wave of dreadful terror realised the two pythons were following. He thought he'd try his one weapon and he let rip with a *TITANIC* fart, so enormous that the trees in the park shook and leaves fell all over the place, the flags by the Surf Club flapped loudly and grass was laid almost dead flat.

THHHHHRRRRRRRRRRRRRRRRRRRRRPPPPPPPP!!!!

Behind him, Gilbert heard a roar.

"PHEWOARRRRRRRRRR!   Gilbert!   Give it a rest, mate, we're not going to eat you!!!! Oh PEWWWWWWW, that's *DISGUSTING!!!!!*

Astonished, Gilbert stopped running and turned round. A few yards away, both Pythons had reared up and each was waving its tail in the face of the other one to clear the air. After a few seconds, they put their heads down on the grass again and moved a bit nearer to Gilbert. Still trembling from the shock, Gilbert waited, realising that the two huge snakes did actually look quite friendly.

"Honest Gilbert, we're not going to eat you!" said one.

"But that's what pythons eat, mice and frogs!" said Gilbert, his voice shaky.

"Oh sure, and we used to," said the other. "But we became vegetarians about a year ago. Much healthier! By the way, I'm Ethelred and this is my wife, Edna."

"Very pleased to meet you," said Gilbert, still feeling very uncertain about this strange turn of events.

"Our pleasure," said Edna. "We were hoping to meet you after hearing about your adventures."

"Vegetarian pythons? I've never heard of vegetarian pythons!" said Gilbert, starting to laugh at the whole silly idea and relaxing in the face of what seemed really friendly snakes.

"Nor had we until a year or so ago," replied Ethelred. "But then I started to get high cholesterol and my blood pressure started going up and the doctor suggested we should try it, so we did and we both feel a whole lot better since then."

"So what do you eat?"

"Well, things like....." And before he'd finished, Ethelred suddenly shot off in the direction of where the vegetable produce stalls had been the day before and a few moments later he returned with a huge potato in his jaws. He dropped it and then did what pythons do with their prey, he wrapped his body around it and squeezed and squeezed and *squeezed* and then relaxed and straightened out.

"See?" said Edna. "Instant mashed potato! Yummy!"

And both snakes took a large mouthful of the creamy raw potato and proceeded to finish it all.

"Excuse us, but we hadn't had breakfast," said Ethelred, wiping his lips with his tail.

"That's definitely better," added Edna. "Now, Gilbert, we want to hear all about your adventures."

Beginning to like his two new friends, Gilbert started to tell them all about his first orbital flight, how he and Percy the Pooping Potoroo had got rid of the burglars and how he had broken the sound barrier at the Fart Propulsion Laboratories at Wagga Wagga.

"That's brilliant!" exclaimed Edna. "But you must be glad to be home now. It's lovely here."

"Well, it was until last night," said Gilbert sadly. "I may have to move."

"Good grief, why?" demanded a shocked Ethelred, and Gilbert

told them about the rampaging rats of the previous night and how frightened he had been.

"So that's what all that squealing was," said Ethelred thoughtfully. "We heard it but couldn't make out what it was. I thought it might have been the train going by and needing a good oiling. But I can understand why you may have to leave."

"We can't have that!" said Edna angrily. "We've only just got to know you! Husband, dear, what shall we do to help Gilbert?"

"I know just the thing," replied Ethelred with a smirk. "Remember, pythons eat rats. They're our staple diet."

"But you said you don't eat rats!" exclaimed Gilbert. "You've become vegetarians!"

"Ah, yes," said Ethelred. "**We** know that and **you** know that, but the rats don't know that! So here's the plan." And he rapidly explained his plan of action to Gilbert who nodded in agreement. It was an excellent plan.

Edna and Ethelred crawled off to their den to sleep a bit and Gilbert returned to his drain hole house to wait until dusk.

That evening, as the sun was setting, that dreadful ratty squealing started again. From the shelter of the pile of leaves, Gilbert watched the horde arrive, knowing from the previous night that the leaves hid his scent from the horrible rats. The army of ugly rodents flooded into the paddock from the roadside and began spreading out looking for food.

But their excited squeals suddenly turned to screeches of horror as Edna and Ethelred appeared at the edge of the field, reared up and moved rapidly at the crowd of rats. The rodents were clearly terrified and the two pythons made it worse by striking at the rats, occasionally biting one and they herded them into the middle of the field, all crammed together trying to escape the pythons.

"Now, Gilbert!" shouted Edna and the two pythons moved sharply away from the mass of frightened rats. Gilbert leaped out from his cover, pointed his little rear end at the middle of the crowd and let rip with a majestic, an awe-inspiring fart, a fart quite capable of blasting him back into orbit if he hadn't positioned himself by a tree root that stopped him from moving.

THHHHRRRRRRRRRRRRRRRRRRRRRRRPPPPPPPP!!

The blast struck the centre of the rat crowd with incredible results. In one vast cloud, the rats flew to the end of the field, across the road, tumbling all over each other, falling sharply into the rocks by the beach and being battered against the stone.

"Well done, mate!" said Edna with a laugh as she and Ethelred joined Gilbert by the tree root.

"Hmmmmmm," said Ethelred. "I have to say, biting some of those rats brought back memories of how good they tasted!"

"Now then, hubby," Edna replied with a small flick of her tail across Ethelred's mouth. "Remember that blood pressure and cholesterol problem. We're vegetarians now. But of course, the rats still don't know that. Not much chance they'll be back, I reckon!" "

And she was right. Never again did Gilbert see a rat at the market site.

7. In Which Gilbert and His Friends Go to the Footie Match

Gilbert had never been to a footie match. The crowds were much too heavy for a small mouse to try and wander around, he knew he'd get stomped on and anyway, there was no way he could actually see the game in such a crowd. So it was rather a surprise to discover that Edna and Ethelred the Vegetarian Pythons were serious footie fans and supporters of the local Coffs Harbour team, the Crushers.

"You mean you actually go and watch the matches?" Gilbert asked in amazement.

"Wouldn't miss it for quids," replied Ethelred and Edna nodded in agreement. "They're our local team anyway, but they're also called the Crushers, so of *course* we support them!"

"But how do you manage it? How do you avoid all the people?"

"No worries," said Edna. "We get to the ground before the people start arriving and we have a nice route round the river bank, so nobody sees us. And we found a place under one of the storage boxes right on the side where's there's a big gap so we can see out and watch the game with nobody near us except when the line judge runs by. Why don't you come this Saturday? It's the Championship final and we're playing the Bellingen Bombers."

"Yes, you should come, Gilbert," Ethelred added. "The prize money is ten thousand dollars and it goes to local charities, so come and support the team!"

"Well, alright," Gilbert said. "Can I bring Percy the Pooping Potoroo?"

"The more the merrier," replied Edna.

Percy the Pooping Potoroo had met the two Pythons a few days ago, though it had taken Gilbert some hard work to persuade him.

"PYTHONS?" shouted Percy in horror. "Great big Potoroo-eating pythons? You've got to be kidding me!" And he shook with huge trembles of panic at the idea.

"Relax, mate, they're vegetarians!" said Gilbert. And although it took twenty minutes of hard work, Percy eventually was able to meet Edna and Ethelred and eventually accepted that he was in no danger and they became good friends.

So that Saturday morning, Percy and Gilbert followed Edna and Ethelred along the river banks, through gullies and hollows and arrived at the footie ground by nine, some hours before the game started. They crawled under the fence and there, on one side opposite the main stands there was a big wooden storage crate with a plank missing along the bottom through which they all sneaked in. That gap gave a splendid view of the field, but until the game started, all four creatures simply went to sleep in the dark shade of the crate.

They woke quickly as the crowds started entering the field and the noise got louder and louder with the excited spectators all anticipating a great game. Gilbert felt the same excitement, even though he'd never seen a footie match before, and with so much money riding on the game, he really hoped the local team would win.

About an hour later, the teams came out onto the field, a band played the national anthem and the game started. Gilbert was entranced! The speed of the running, the furious tackles, massive kicks and fast passing all had him jumping with enthusiasm and Percy was just the same. Edna and Ethelred were much quieter and just watched the game calmly, but when the Coffs Harbour Crushers scored the first try, they waved their heads wildly and hissed in appreciation. Percy got so excited that he started to poop, but Edna flicked her tail at him and threw him outside before he really got started, so Percy ran up and down the side of the storage crate, leaving lines of Potoroo poop, but luckily the grass was quite thick there, so it was unlikely anyone would see the poop and start to investigate.

At half time, the Crushers were in the lead by three tries to two and that's how it remained most of the way through the second half. But with five minutes to go, the Bellingen Bombers scored a try to even up the score and Gilbert started to get anxious as the minutes ticked away. He really wanted that $10,000 to go to Coffs Harbour.

The Crushers worked their way up into the opponent's half but still seemed a long way from scoring and Gilbert began to despair of his team winning. But then, with just seconds to go, there was a collision between two players only about twenty metres from where the four friends were watching, and the referee blew his whistle and pointed.

"What's happening?" asked Gilbert who couldn't work out what was going on.

"The ref has awarded our blokes a penalty kick," replied Ethelred.

"What does that mean?"

"Our bloke will kick the ball and it has to go over the bar between the two uprights. If he does that, we get three points and we win the match," explained Ethelred.

"He's got to do it, he's *GOT* to!" squeaked Gilbert.

"Here's hoping," Edna said as the kicker carefully placed the ball on a small mound of dirt. "It's quite a long kick and there's some twisting wind around. It's not going to be easy."

"I know!" shouted Gilbert and jumped up and out of the crate. "I'll make sure!"

"No!" said Edna firmly. "I know what you're thinking of and that's not right! It's cheating."

"But we need the money," said Gilbert and he raced out of the crate and scampered the twenty metres or so to where the kicker had stepped back from the ball and was standing motionless as he prepared for the kick.

Gilbert flew past him and along to the ball. He leaped up onto the ball and found where the laces had been tightly done up. He clamped down on the laces with all four claws and his teeth, knowing this was going to be really difficult. He heard the kicker start his run up, the crowd started roaring in encouragement and then **SLAM!!!!!**

It was worse than when the Fart Reheat had cut in on the jet trolley at the Fart Propulsion Laboratories in Wagga Wagga, it was explosive, massive, but Gilbert managed to hang on as the ball flew into the air. He looked ahead and saw that he was flying in the right direction, but it felt to him that he was probably too low and the kick wasn't going to get over the bar. He took a deep breath and let out a mid-sized but forceful fart.

THHHHHHHHHHHRRRRRRRRRRRPPPPPPPPPPP!

The ball lifted about two metres and accelerated sharply, but Gilbert realised he had misjudged his position on the ball. He was flying a bit too far to the left, straight at the upright and he frantically tried to point his rear end a bit to the left and he let out a small corrective fart **thhhhrrrppp** but it was too late and the ball hit the upright. It bounced to the right, following the line of the horizontal bar, struck the right hand upright, dropped and struck the crossbar and just dropped over it and into touch. Dazed and battered, Gilbert let go of the ball, dropped to the grass and nearly blacked out. But he felt triumphant. His side had won! He was thrilled to bits!

But he suddenly realised there was somebody standing over him. He shook his head to clear his vision and realised it was the referee who was standing above him, so huge that he almost blacked out the sky. The referee crouched down and glared at Gilbert.

"So you must be Gilbert the Farting Mouse, eh?" said the referee in a deep, resounding voice.

Gilbert could only nod his head weakly.

"We've heard all about you," continued the referee, "and we're all very proud of what you've done to help people, but this is not good."

Feeling ashamed, Gilbert nodded his head again.

"It's cheating," said the referee. "And we don't like cheating in sports."

Gilbert wanted the ground to open up and swallow him, he felt so embarrassed.

"So I've cancelled that penalty kick and the score remains even. But with the cheating attempt, the Crushers should really forfeit the game and be declared the losers."

Gilbert nodded, wishing the torture would end.

"But what we've agreed is that the ball might have gone over if you hadn't tried to fart it over and got the direction wrong," continued the referee. "So instead of forfeiting the match, we've agreed to let the score remain even and the prize money will be divided between the two towns."

Gilbert felt a little better, but still wished he could vanish.

"Okay, Gilbert, so run along and don't do anything like that again, will you?"

Gilbert shook his head.

"But I hope you'll come to the games regularly, Gilbert. We all think you're a pretty good bloke, really."

And with that, the referee stood up and walked away, leaving Gilbert to run as hard as he could back to where his friends were waiting.

"Reckon you got off lightly there, you silly mouse!" said Percy the Pooping Potoroo.

"I'll say!" agreed Gilbert. "But I feel a complete idiot."

"Well, let's forget it," said Ethelred. "We'll wait until the crowd's gone, then we can check the place out for some good tucker. I saw somebody drop a whole container of potato wedges earlier on. I *love* potato wedges."

"And if we're lucky, there'll be sour cream with it," added Edna, flicking her tongue out in anticipation. "And there'll be lots of stuff for you blokes, too. Plenty of hot dogs and hamburgers and all that yucky meat stuff!"

And she was right. After waiting till the stands were empty, the Pythons did indeed find a carton of potato wedgies and sour cream while Gilbert and Percy were able to dine in style on hot dogs and hamburgers.

Gilbert decided that all in all, it had been a splendid day but he would never forget how ashamed he had been at trying to cheat, even if it had been in a good cause.

8. In Which Gilbert Saves the Sydney Hobart Yacht Race

Gilbert had really enjoyed Christmas this year. The weather had been perfect, all sunny, warm and calm and he had invited his friends together for a special Christmas dinner. Percy the Pooping Potoroo had come and brought some fresh Camembert Cheese that he had lifted from the house of the rich young men where he and Gilbert had once defeated the burglars. He said the two men had held another party for about thirty friends, but they'd all decided to head for the beach at some point, leaving lots of yummy stuff on the table. Edna and Ethelred turned up carrying two really huge potatoes they'd found and they crushed them into mashed spuds, while Gilbert had also found some potato wedgies for them. Gilbert had been collecting for a day or two as well, so he had some smoked salmon sushi, a couple of large pieces of curried chicken and a whole slice of hamburger that had fallen out of somebody's picnic basket. Fiona the Crab ambled up from the beach carrying two fresh prawns and so everybody had a right royal pig-out before strolling down to the beach where they said hello to Karen the Octopus floating a few metres into the water, and waved to Wilma and Warwick, the two whales who were heading south to Tasmania again.

Gilbert had slept very well, having avoided the seriously fart-causing foods and only had a very small nibble of macadamia nut for dessert. The next morning he sneaked into the Yacht Club by the jetty and watched the start of the Sydney-Hobart Yacht Race on the club's television set. There weren't many people in there to worry about as most were out on their own boats, so Gilbert enjoyed himself watching all the boats milling around in Sydney Harbour and finally getting started, sailing in long lines out of the Harbour, past the Heads before turning south for Hobart. The weather girl on the television sounded pessimistic;

"Forecasts are for very light winds," she said. "Possibly even having a period of no wind at all, leaving all the boats becalmed."

But Gilbert wasn't worried about that, as he was planning to spend the day at his beach house, listening to the surf and waiting for the next market day which would be wonderful, he knew, because all the tourists were in Coffs Harbour, and they'd be flocking to the market as they left the beach.

But early in the morning, asleep in the beach house, he was woken by a piercing whistle. He recognised the sound from when Fiona had used it to call the two whales to help him, so he ran outside and sure enough, there was Fiona waiting on the sand.

"G'Day, Fiona," he said. "How would you be?"

"I'm right, Gilbert," she replied. "But we need your help. The boat race is in trouble."

"But that's several hundred kilometres south of here!" protested Gilbert. "How am I supposed to get down there?"

"In a very special way, mate," said Fiona. "Better grab your emergency ration pack, we're going to need your special talents."

Luckily, Gilbert had brought his little back pack with some macadamia nuts to the beach house, because he always carried it with him in case of emergencies. He raced back inside and strapped the pack on his back and returned to Wilma. She had walked down to the water's edge and she emitted an enormous whistle. A few minutes later, Gilbert saw a pair of water spouts about a hundred metres off the shore.

"This is Ken and Katrina. Can you get us out there?" said Fiona, waving her eyestalks back and forth.

"No worries," said Gilbert and waited till Fiona had clasped two claws round his neck, took a deep breath and let loose with a small propellant fart **thrrrrrrpppppppp** that launched them into the air and flew a perfect trajectory to land on the back of the leading whale.

"G'day, I'm Ken," said the whale. "Hang on to my fin, 'cos we're really going to have to move, okay?"

And with that, he accelerated along the surface at a rate that Gilbert found really exhilarating, though a bit scary at the same time.

"So what's going on?" he asked Fiona as they flew along the sea surface.

"Total lack of any wind at all," she replied. "All the boats have come to a complete stop, nothing's happening, everybody's really hacked off, crew, spectators, television companies, it's a disaster!"

"So how long will it take us to get there?"

"About twenty-four hours. We'll be there in the morning."

"You mean we have to sleep on Ken's back? How are we going to hang on all night?"

"No worries," she said, clacking her claws in amusement. "A pile of us rigged the harness for that. Look!" And she pointed at the back of the fin and sure enough, there was a harness made of seaweed big enough for both of them and a neat shelter made of a coconut.

"But what if dives under the surface?" Gilbert really wasn't sure about this whole thing.

"He won't," Fiona assured him. "You'd be surprised how often the whales do this transport thing for us! They've got used to knowing when they have to stay on the surface!"

Comforted, Gilbert settled down to enjoying the speedy transit along the sea, watching the coast of Australia in the distance and by nightfall he fell asleep safely folded inside his harness on Ken's back.

When he woke just before dawn, the silence was the first thing that hit him. The sea was flat calm and there was not a ripple anywhere to be seen except the disturbance from the movements of Ken the whale.

"And this is the problem," said the voice of Fiona behind him. "Sailing boats don't do too well when it's like this!"

"I can imagine," replied Gilbert, speaking softly in the immense quiet that surrounded them.

The sun started to appear and slowly the surrounding scene became clearer. All around him, Gilbert saw sailing boats lying motionless in the sea, sails drooping like wet handkerchiefs. Gilbert felt a change of direction from Ken the whale.

"He's moving to the north of the fleet," said Fiona. "And here's Katrina, we'll need her for support."

Gilbert watched the second whale approach and began swimming alongside Ken as they moved to the north of the becalmed fleet of sailboats.

"A single fart isn't the answer," Gilbert said. "That will just move the boats for a few minutes. I think this needs a Phased Fart approach."

"You're right," Fiona replied. "I'll talk to Ken and Katrina." She ran along Ken's back to his head and they engaged in soft discussions for a few moments before she returned.

"Okay," she said. "We think the boats need a couple of soft blasts to wake them up and get moving, then a big one and leave that for a few minutes, get them all downwind and then the King Hit Fart. Okay with you?"

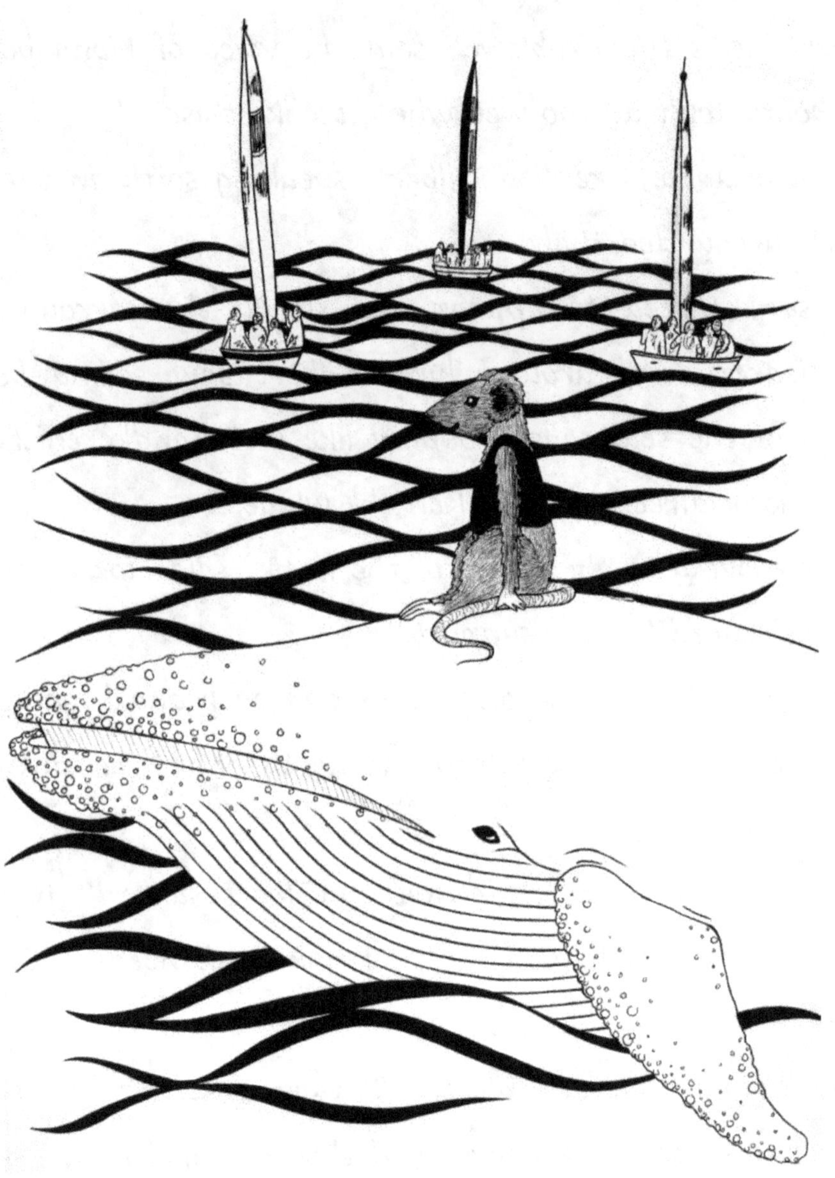

"Give me a moment," Gilbert replied and took his backpack off and opened it. He selected a small macadamia nut and chewed it slowly and then announced, "Okay, Phase One."

He directed his little rear end at the fleet of boats and let out three small but tuneful farts, each a little stronger than the previous one:

Thrrrrppppppp!!

Thrrrrrrppppppppppppppp!

Thrrrrrrrrrppppppppppppppppppppp!

He waited and watched and then things started happening. Sails started flapping and as they did, people began appearing on the decks of the sailboats and much shouting and yelling could be heard from all the boats. People began pulling on ropes and on each boat, somebody leaped at the steering wheel as the boats began slowly moving. Sails started to fill out and the boats began moving faster and lots of people on the boats began cheering.

Gilbert waited and watched and when the boats were all in motion, turned round again, presented his rear to the south, hung on to the harness attached to Ken's dorsal fin and this time emitted a much more forceful blast:

THRRRRRRRRRRRPPPPPPPPPPPPPPPPPPPPPP!!!!!!!!!!

Immediately south of the two whales, the sea surface began to get agitated and waves blew up, white foam covered the surface and it got quite rough.

It took a few moments for the gale force to reach the fleet but when it did, the boats took off and accelerated, crews began loading their massive spinnaker sails and letting them out and the colours were beautiful and exciting.

"Give it ten minutes!" shouted Fiona who was jumping up and down with glee. "And that should do it!"

Gilbert realised that Katrina had moved alongside Ken and they had turned sideways on to the direction of wind.

"That's to hold you in place," Fiona called. "Otherwise they could be forced back up north when you let rip with the Big One!"

As Gilbert was watching the results of his efforts, a small speck appeared from the south, quite high in the sky and it was coming directly to the two whales. As it grew bigger, Gilbert saw it was a bird and at first he thought it was a seagull, but it got closer and closer and it was obviously too big for a seagull. For a while, as it approached the whales, it was obviously being buffeted around severely, but then the wind eased as it passed south and a huge white albatross landed on the back of Ken.

"G'day," the albatross said. "My name's Alphonse, and I've been spotting the weather for you further south. I tell you what, that's some storm you farted up there, Gilbert!"

"Well, thanks, Alphonse! It seems to have done the trick. So what's happening further south?"

"There's a cool change coming through," Alphonse said, starting to smooth his feathers after his stormy ride. "The winds will begin picking up about fifty kilometres south, so she'll be apples down there. I reckon you need one more king-size, humungous, rip-snorting fart to get them there."

"No worries," said Gilbert. "About now?"

"About now," agreed Alphonse the Albatross. "Anytime you're ready."

"Give me a moment, I need recharging," Gilbert said, taking out a really large macadamia nut from his bag and starting to chomp on it. Within a minute, he'd finished it and started jumping up and down to speed up the effect. "Okay, ready when you are," he shouted to Ken and Katrina.

The two whales lined up across the direction of the coming blast to hold Gilbert in place, he grabbed the harness again, pointed his rear down to the south and really let it all happen.

THHHHHHHRRRRRRRRRRRRRRRRRPPPPPPPPP!!

The sea flattened out under the force of the cyclone Gilbert had created. The wind howled like a crazed banshee and clouds above became torn into small wisps. The storm raced south, but by the time it reached the fleet that was now several kilometres away, it had become just a strong wind and all the yachts moved sharply to use it and began flying down the coast.

"That'll do it," Alphonse the Albatross said and spread his enormous wings. "I'll head down there and keep an eye on things."

"Thanks, mate," said Gilbert as the albatross took off and soared away to the south.

"Well done, Gilbert!" called Katrina as the two whales turned north again. "We'll have you home tomorrow!"

And they did. Fiona slipped off into the sea about five kilometres from Coffs Harbour, saying she needed the exercise and when Gilbert saw the jetty of the sailing club, he performed a perfect fart-leap for the club house and crept into the television room just in time to hear the commentator saying how baffled the meteorologists were at the wind storm that had blown up and ended the awful silence and windless conditions.

"But whatever the reasons," said the commentator, "all the crews are very grateful as are all the spectators and sailing enthusiasts around the world. The race has been saved and now we can all look forward to seeing who gets line honours and handicap honours in this world famous yacht race."

Smiling to himself, Gilbert found his way back to his drain home and settled down to rest, knowing he had performed a great service to the world.